True Blue

Adapted by Laurie McElroy

Based on the series created by Michael Poryes and Rich Correll & Barry O'Brien

Part One is based on the episode, "Cuffs Will Keep Us Together," Written by Steven Peterman

Part Two is based on the episode, "Me And Rico Down By The School Yard," Written by Heather Wordham

New York

Printed in the United States of America

First Edition
1 3 5 7 9 10 8 6 4 2

Library of Congress Control Number: 2007905284
ISBN 978-1-4231-0869-6

PART ONE

Chapter One

Miley Stewart and Lilly Truscott were dressed for gym class and stretching out on the high school athletic field. Miley was already dreading what was in store. "I hate flag football," she complained. "It's just one more sport where I get picked last. And you want to know why?"

Lilly snorted. "'Cause you stink?"

Miley glared at her.

"Or, 'cause you're pretty and all the other girls are jealous?" Lilly asked in a singsong voice with a sweet smile.

"Nice save," Miley said sarcastically. "Look, I know I'm not good, but I'm not horrible."

Just then their gym teacher, Mrs. McDermott, walked across the field. "Look alive, Stewart," she said, tossing Miley the football.

Instead of catching the ball, Miley threw her hands up to protect herself and tried to jump out of the way. But she didn't even do that right—the ball hit her in the head.

Lilly gave her friend a knowing look.

"Okay, I'm horrible," Miley admitted. "But you don't know how it feels always being the last one picked because nobody wants 'Stinky Stewart.'"

"Hey, last year in soccer I wasn't picked until practically the end," Lilly answered, trying to sympathize. But she couldn't really relate. Lilly was a great athlete.

"You had a broken collarbone," Miley reminded her. "And you still got picked ahead of me! I just wish one time some miracle would happen, and I wouldn't get picked last."

Mrs. McDermott crossed the field again. She pointed to a tough-looking girl named Joannie Palumbo and then to Lilly. "Palumbo. Truscott. You're captains. Pick your teams!"

"Yes!" Miley clapped her hands excitedly. "Yes! Yes!" she cried, throwing her arms around Lilly. "Finally a captain who'll pick me first!"

Joannie leaned in. "Doesn't matter who you pick, Truscott," she said with a hiss. "Your team is going down."

Lilly planted her hands on her hips and narrowed her eyes. She and Joannie had been rivals since elementary school. "In your dreams, Palumbo."

"You've been trying to beat me at something since the second grade." Joannie sneered. "News flash: never gonna happen." She turned to Miley. "Hey, Stinky, how you doing?"

"Not bad," Miley answered, then realized she had just been insulted. "Hey!"

Mrs. McDermott walked up carrying a football. "Let's go, ladies!" she yelled. "Pick your teams. You're slower than my husband in the bathroom." She sighed. "I curse the day he put that plasma screen in there."

Miley and Lilly, looking confused, watched her walk off. A plasma screen in the bathroom?

The rest of the class lined up, waiting to be picked.

"Pick first, Truscott," Joannie said.

"You're gonna need all the help you can get."

Miley strutted to Lilly's side with her head high. "She's not the one who's going to need help."

"Oh, yeah?" Joannie challenged.

"Yeah!" Lilly answered.

"Darn right, yeah!" Miley added confidently. "You're going down, Phony Joannie."

"Who smells like week-old bologna—" Lilly said with a smile.

Miley kept the rhyme going. "That's been in your locker all alone-y."

"Right next to that . . . that . . ." Lilly stammered.

Miley jumped in. "Melted ice-cream cone-y."

Lilly was impressed. "Oooh, girl, you are in the zone-y!" she said to Miley.

Miley shrugged.

But Joannie wasn't intimidated; in fact, she was just getting started. "Yo, Salt-n-Pepa," she said, getting in Lilly's face. "You wanna bet on it?"

"Does she!" Miley answered. "How about winning captain . . ." she pointed to Lilly, ". . . gets to give losing captain . . ." she pointed to Joannie, ". . . a little haircut?"

Lilly's eyes widened in horror. What was Miley getting her into?

"You're on!" Joannie exclaimed, shaking her head. Her long brown curls flew back and forth. She reached out to shake Lilly's hand.

Lilly touched her own long blonde hair. She didn't want to lose it. "Or," she said slowly, trying to buy some time, "we could just bet a quarter. 'Cause you know it's just about the fun of competition."

Joannie smiled back. "No, it's really about the fun of me kicking your butt. . . ." She leaned in with a smirk. "Again. Yeah!"

Now Lilly was mad. The game hadn't even started yet, and Joannie was celebrating her victory. "That's it! You're on!" Lilly snapped. To seal the deal, she shook Joannie's hand.

"Go ahead, Lilly," Miley prodded. "Pick away, make my day, everything's gonna be okay—"

Lilly pointed to the best player she could think of. "Kowalski."

Miley gasped. Had she heard wrong? Had Lilly just picked someone other than her? "What'd you say?" Miley asked.

But Lilly didn't hear her. She was too busy sizing up the girls, deciding whom she'd pick next.

* * *

Five minutes later, Miley and another girl named Sarah were the only two players still waiting to be picked. Miley glared daggers at her best friend.

Sarah had her nose in a book, as usual. She looked up and suddenly noticed that she was standing next to Miley. "Wow. Isn't it funny how it always comes down to the two of us?" she asked.

"Yeah, hilarious," Miley said sarcastically.

"Well, I hope you don't get picked last this time," Sarah said generously.

"Yeah, me too," Miley said, loud enough for Lilly to hear.

A football rolled in front of the two girls. Sarah dropped her book and picked it up. "Careful, you almost hit that anthill!" she called. "Even these tiny creatures are very important to our ecosystem."

Joannie checked out the two remaining

players and laughed. "Pick your poison, Truscott. You're gettin' a buzz cut either way."

"I pick . . ." Lilly's eyes darted from Miley to Sarah and back to Miley again.

Sarah kicked the football. Everyone watched, totally amazed, as it sailed across the field. If this was part of the game, she would have made a field goal. Sarah could kick!

". . . Sarah!" Lilly finished.

"Good luck, Stinky," Sarah said kindly. "Bye!"

Miley stomped over to Joannie's team, glaring at Sarah and Lilly as she passed them. She couldn't believe she had been picked last—again!

Chapter Two

That night, Hannah Montana was onstage, finishing the chorus to her last song, "True Friend." Her fans cheered. They wanted another encore, but Miley had already given them two. It was time to say good night.

"I love you all! I wish I could stay all night," she said to her fans as she ran offstage. Backstage, she was less enthusiastic. She threw her microphone toward a stagehand. "Let's get out of here," she muttered to her father, Robby Stewart.

Mr. Stewart was in his Hannah Montana–manager disguise: a big mustache and a hat. "Darlin', are you still upset about what happened with you and Lilly?" he asked.

"No, of course not. Why would you say that?" Miley snapped.

"Well, you don't normally introduce 'True Friend' as a touching little song about a two-faced backstabber," he answered.

"Just my way of keeping things fresh," Miley said with a shrug. "You know I'm an artist, that's what I do."

Mr. Stewart wasn't buying Miley's story. "Well, I'm a dad, and knowing that's a hunk a hooey is what I do."

"Am I going to get another lecture?" Miley asked.

"Maybe later," he replied. "Right now,

I've got to get this dang mustache off."

On Lilly's way backstage, she passed Mr. Stewart. She was wearing a metallic red wig. When she hung out with Hannah Montana, Lilly called herself Lola Luftnagle and wore funky clothes and makeup.

"Lola, be thankful you don't have to wear one of these," Mr. Stewart said, pointing to his mustache. "This thing's itchier than a baboon's butt at a flea circus."

Lilly gazed at him blankly. What could she say to that?

"Well, look who showed up," Miley said. "Were the other concerts in town sold out? Because I know you wouldn't have picked mine first. Or second. Or *last*!"

"Hey, I was going to pick you until you started that haircut thing," Lilly said. "And what's the big deal anyway? I won! Want to share the trophy?" She reached into her purse and pulled out a clump of brown, curly hair. "I couldn't have done it without your three fumbles," Lilly said with a smile, trying to coax Miley out of being mad.

Miley really did not want to be reminded about her fumbles. "It's a stupid game!" she yelled. "The ball's not even round!"

Just then, Traci Van Horne ran backstage with a couple of friends. "Hannah!" she called out, smiling. Traci was a rich girl who liked to hang out with Hannah, the pop star, and had no idea she was also Miley, an ordinary teen.

"Hey, guys!" Miley said, giving Traci air kisses. "What's up, Traci?"

"You just get better and better!" Traci gushed. "I loved the little backstabbing quip. So funny!" She leaned in to whisper. "That wasn't about me, was it?"

"No, no, no! Of course not," Miley said, making sure Lilly could hear. "I know I can always count on *you,*" she said to Traci.

"Come on," Lilly said quietly so only Miley could hear. "You're not going to stay mad at me forever, are you?"

"I think I'm a little more mature than that," Miley replied. Then she spoke loud enough for the whole group to hear. "I've got five empty seats in my limo. So, I pick you, you, you, and you." She pointed to everyone but Lilly. "Let's go."

"Wait," Lilly said. "That's only four."

"Oh, right. I forgot about Fern," Miley answered.

"Who's Fern?" Lilly asked.

"My new best friend." Miley grabbed a silk plant and started to leave.

Lilly was totally confused. "That's a ficus," she said, watching Miley leave.

"A ficus named Fern!" Miley said defensively, hugging the plant. "She's getting the window seat. Oh, yeah!"

Miley slept late the next morning, so her brother, Jackson, had the kitchen to himself at breakfast. He had a box of his favorite cereal and a carton of milk, but he needed a bowl. He searched through a sink full of dirty dishes and grabbed a spoon. A bowl came out with it—the spoon was cemented inside by whatever food had hardened in the bowl. He dropped it with a grimace. Gross!

If Jackson wanted breakfast, he was going to have to get creative. He poured the milk inside the cereal box, shook it, lifted the box over his head, and turned it upside down. It was a brilliant plan. In fact, he might have invented something new—

drinkable cereal. He was thinking of names for his new product when Mr. Stewart came into the kitchen with a basket of laundry.

"Jackson!" he yelled.

"What?" Jackson asked with his mouth full. "I'm eating over the sink." He pointed to the stack of dirty dishes.

"That's not a sink," Mr. Stewart said, putting the laundry down on the table. "It's a toxic-waste dump. I've been asking you for three days to get these dishes done. Look at this," he said, picking up a greenish glob from one of the dishes. "This spinach has hair on it."

"That's not spinach," Jackson answered. "That's a piece of chicken."

"Neeaaahh!" Mr. Stewart screamed, throwing it back.

"Look, Dad, I'll get to it," Jackson assured him.

"When?" Mr. Stewart asked. "When this stuff up and crawls away?"

"Do you think it could do that?" Jackson said. "'Cause that would be so cool!"

Mr. Stewart threw his hands up in the air in frustration. "That's it. I ask you to do the dishes, I get green chicken. I ask you to separate the whites in the laundry, I get green underwear." Mr. Stewart pulled a pair of boxer shorts out of the laundry basket. They had been dyed bright green.

Jackson didn't see what the problem was. So there were a few dirty dishes, and a couple of whites might have gotten thrown into the washing machine with the colors. No need to make a huge deal about it. "Hey, what are you worried about? Nobody's gonna see them unless you do that sunrise yoga out on the deck again," Jackson said. "Talk about your 'neeaaahh!'"

he added, imitating his father's scream.

"It centers me, boy!" Mr. Stewart said firmly. "I shouldn't have to tell you things over and over again, Jackson. You are not ten years old."

Jackson rolled his eyes and popped a handful of soggy cereal in his mouth. "Okay, okay, I'm sorry," he said insincerely.

Mr. Stewart wasn't laughing. "No, you're not. You're just saying that because you're afraid I'm going to ground you."

"C'mon, Dad. I apologized. You want me to mean it, too?" Jackson shook his head in disbelief.

"Yes. Jackson, I want you to hear me when I'm talking to you. And since you never listen, I'm just not going to waste my breath anymore."

"What's that supposed to mean?" Jackson asked.

Mr. Stewart didn't answer. He checked a cabinet. It was empty.

"Dad?"

Another cabinet had a clean cake pan inside. Mr. Stewart grabbed another box of cereal out of the cupboard and filled the pan.

"Ohhh, the silent treatment?" Jackson asked, finally catching on. "That's my punishment? You're gonna stop telling me what to do. Sweet!" He pumped his fist in the air. This was going to be fun!

Mr. Stewart grabbed the milk and added it to his cereal.

"I mean, that's a very good choice," Jackson continued. "Boy, I sure hope I learn! Even if it takes a week, a month, you take your time." He nudged his father's arm. "This is important," he said earnestly. Then he ran out of the room laughing while Mr. Stewart calmly ate his cake pan of cereal.

Chapter Three

Later that afternoon, Mr. Stewart was hanging out on the living room couch, watching football and eating popcorn.

Jackson ran down the stairs. "Dad, why didn't you tell me the Titans' game started?"

Mr. Stewart grabbed the remote and turned up the volume.

"Ohhh, right. Daddy no talkie Jackson," Jackson said in a baby voice. Then the game caught his attention. "Vince is out of the pocket!" he yelled.

"Go, baby, go!" Mr. Stewart shouted toward the TV.

"Look! He broke a tackle!" Jackson exclaimed.

"C'mon. C'mon. Take it to the house, V-dawg!" Mr. Stewart yelled, not taking his eyes off the television.

Touchdown!

Jackson leapt over the back of the couch and landed next to his father. "Touchdown!" he cried, raising his hand for a high five. "Give it to me."

Mr. Stewart's attention was completely focused on the television.

"Give it to me," Jackson said again. But his father didn't even look at him. "Oh, come on. Come *on*!" Jackson pleaded, getting right into his dad's face.

Mr. Stewart didn't blink, not until the phone rang. He picked it up, still pretending that Jackson wasn't there. "Hello?" A smile spread across his face. "You're kidding. That's great."

"What's great?" Jackson asked.

"We're tickled pinker than a pig in a purple prom dress," Mr. Stewart said, ignoring Jackson. "We'll be there."

"What pig?" Jackson asked as soon as his father hung up. "Dad, why are we tickled?"

"Hey, Mile!" Mr. Stewart yelled upstairs. "Get down here. Got some great news!"

Jackson hated not knowing what was going on. "Okay, now who's acting like the ten-year-old?" he asked his father. "I'll tell you who. You. That's who. You, you, you, you, you." Jackson started poking his father in the stomach, trying to get a rise out of him, but Mr. Stewart didn't react.

Jackson threw himself across his father's lap and started sucking his thumb like a baby. Then he covered his eyes. "Peeka*you*!" Jackson sat up again and grabbed his father's bottom lip. He pulled it up and down while he talked for him. "Hey, look at me. I'm a ten-year-old with big sideburns and ten-year-old big—"

Mr. Stewart stared straight ahead the whole time.

Jackson totally lost it now. He jumped to his feet. "You're the ten-year-old! You're the ten-year-old!" he repeated, jumping up and down on the couch. "You are! You are!"

But it was no fun fighting with someone who didn't fight back. Jackson dived over the couch and headed for the stairs, stopping to turn around and point at his father. "Youuuuuu," he said in a drawn-out whisper, just before running up the stairs.

Miley passed him on her way down. "I'd ask why Jackson's gone squirrelly, but then I'd have to pretend that I actually care," she said. "What's the news?"

"I just got a call from Nashville," Mr. Stewart said, turning away from the game. "Guess what single just won a Silver Boot for Best Country/Pop Crossover?"

Miley gasped. "'True Friend' won a Booty?"

"You got it!" Mr. Stewart cried.

Miley screamed and gave him a high five. "I can't believe it! This has always been my dream. Being on national television, holding my own Booty."

"Well, get ready, darling, because tomorrow night, live via satellite, that dream is coming true!"

Miley screamed again.

"I'm happy for ya, baby. You know, it's a night you'll never forget." Mr. Stewart walked over to a shelf and picked up a statue of a silver boot wearing a cowboy hat. "I know I never get tired of looking at my own Booty."

"This is so awesome!" Miley exclaimed, heading for the door. "I have got to go tell—"

"Lilly," her father said, finishing her sentence.

Miley suddenly stopped. In her excitement she had forgotten that she was mad at Lilly. "No, I have lots of other BFFs I could tell," she said. "Well, BFs . . ." Miley felt her father's eyes on her back. "Okay, fine, Fs," she said, turning around. "Would you stop torturing me?"

The phone rang as Miley closed the door behind her. Mr. Stewart checked the caller

ID and threw the phone on the couch without answering.

Jackson stood on the deck with his cell phone pressed to his ear. "Answer the phone!" he yelled.

Mr. Stewart calmly opened the refrigerator.

"It could be an emergency!" Jackson exclaimed, coming into the house. "Okay, you wanna play? You wanna play hardball?" he asked, still talking into his phone. "It's on! Like soy sauce on a wonton. You're going to talk to me," he said with a determined glare.

Chapter Four

Oliver Oken had ridden his bicycle to the beach. Instead of his usual lock, he had another tool to make sure his ride didn't get stolen. "Yo, Zack. Check it out," he said, pulling a pair of handcuffs out of his back pocket and using them to attach his bike to the rack.

"Awesome!" Zack exclaimed.

"I know!" Oliver bumped fists with his friend.

"Oliver, I have amazing news!" Miley cried, running up between them.

"So do I. My mom made detective and gave me her old handcuffs! Check it out." Oliver pointed to his bike and waited for Miley to tell him how cool that was. "Huh? Huh?" he prodded.

"Yeah. Great. Terrific," Miley said flatly. She pulled Oliver aside so Zack wouldn't hear. "Hannah won a Silver Boot for Best Country/Pop Crossover!" She squealed and started jumping up and down.

Oliver just stood there, watching her.

"Why aren't you happy-dancing?" Miley asked. He was supposed to jump up and down with her, didn't he know that?

"'Cause I'm not a girl," he said. "And guys don't happy-dance."

"Well, could you at least act a little more excited?" Miley asked, totally annoyed.

This was huge news! Why wasn't Oliver happy for her?

"You weren't excited for me," Oliver said.

"You locked your bike with handcuffs!" Miley shouted.

Zack was still checking out Oliver's new bike lock. "And it's awesome!" he cried.

"Thank you!" Oliver replied, pointing at Zack and then tapping his chest. Zack was being a true friend. Then Oliver turned back to Miley. "You know, if you want a girl's reaction, just go make up with Lilly."

Miley crossed her arms over her chest. "I don't need to make up with Lilly, I have you. Now come on, let's go," she said, grabbing Oliver's arm.

"Where are we going?" Oliver asked.

"To get our nails done," Miley said. Do I have to tell him *everything*? she thought. It made perfect sense to her—award, award show, manicure. Lilly would have known that.

Oliver took a giant step back. "We can't just try that happy-dance thing?" he asked, jumping up and down halfheartedly.

"No. Too late!" Miley grabbed his arm again. "Let's go."

Jackson was sitting on a kitchen stool next to a huge guy wearing a black leather jacket and a do-rag. He was a tattoo artist named Arlo, and he was covered in tattoos. Jackson had asked him to come to the house. Jackson was sure that if he threatened to get a tattoo, his father would talk to him again. This better work, Jackson thought. He was more than a little scared of Arlo.

Arlo showed Jackson a scorpion tattoo

on his left arm—his hugely muscled left arm.

"Your mom must be so proud," Jackson said nervously.

Mr. Stewart walked in the front door with a newspaper and sat down on the couch.

Jackson sat up taller and spoke loud enough for his father to hear. "I want it right here," he said, pointing to his shoulder. "In big letters, 'I Hate Dad.' And put a little barbwire around it."

"Are you sure you don't want to check out some of my flower patterns?" Arlo asked. Jackson didn't exactly look like the barbed-wire type to him.

"Just barbwire me, baby!" Jackson insisted.

"Okay," Arlo said with a shrug. "I just need some parental consent."

Mr. Stewart was calmly reading his newspaper and not paying any attention to the scene being acted out for him.

"No problem." Jackson turned to his father. "Hey, Dad, if you don't want me to get a tattoo, you might want to speak up."

"Jackson!" Mr. Stewart said, hitting his newspaper.

"Yeah?" Jackson asked hopefully.

But Mr. Stewart had been talking to himself. "President Andrew blank. Seven across," he said, reaching for a pencil to fill in the crossword puzzle. "This is too easy."

Jackson turned to Arlo. "Okay, Arlo," he said loudly for his father's benefit. "Needle me."

Arlo slapped Jackson's arm, then swabbed it with disinfectant.

"Yup, I'm really gonna do it," Jackson said. "Even though it's dangerous . . ." He looked over at his father.

Mr. Stewart didn't even seem to notice.

". . . and permanent," Jackson added.

Arlo turned on his needle. It started to buzz like an angry bee.

Jackson eyed the needle's sharp point. His eyes darted nervously from the needle to his father and back again. "Here it comes. . . . It's almost breaking skin. . . ."

Mr. Stewart turned to the comics. "Oh, Marmaduke, you are one funny dog," he said with a laugh.

"Hello!" Jackson yelled. "About to get marked for life here."

Arlo tightened his grip on Jackson's arm.

"Ow!" Jackson said, totally panicked.

"Hold still!" Arlo told him.

The needle was about to break Jackson's skin. "Get away from me with that thing!" he yelled, jumping off the stool. He turned to Mr. Stewart. "What kind of a father are you?"

Mr. Stewart shook his head and chuckled, still reading the paper.

Jackson raced upstairs.

"Hey, man, look at this," Mr. Stewart said to Arlo, pointing to the comics. "Crazy dog thinks he can drive."

An hour later, Miley and Oliver sat at a table at Rico's Surf Shop. Oliver couldn't stop looking at his nails. "You know, that second coat really made a difference."

"I told ya!" Miley said, checking them out. Then her eyes focused on the totally cute boy walking by. "Omigosh, don't you think Richard Bruce has the most amazing eyes?"

Oliver glanced up. "I know. And that blue top he's wearing really makes them pop." Suddenly Oliver heard the words coming out of his mouth and realized he sounded just like Lilly. Miley was turning him into a girl! "What am I saying?" he asked.

Lilly walked by, hitting the back of Miley's chair with her surfboard. She glared at Miley and then smiled sweetly at Oliver. "Hey, Oliver, do you want to go surfing?"

"Yes!" Oliver cried, jumping to his feet and pumping out his chest. "Because I'm a guy. And guys wanna surf in deep water full of sharks." He held his arms out wide. "Big, huge, nasty guy sharks!"

Lilly was focused on his fingernails—his *painted* fingernails. "Are you wearing a clear polish?" she asked.

"It's called buff," Oliver said defensively, pulling his hands back in. He puffed out his chest again and deepened his voice. "Buff, like me. Let's go!"

"Oliver, you can't go with her. The awards are tonight. You have to help me with my hair," Miley said sweetly. She turned to Lilly and added coolly, "I won a Booty."

"Good," Lilly snapped. "You could use one."

Miley gasped. "How rude! Come on, we're leaving. You're coming with me, Oliver."

"No, you're coming with me," Lilly said, grabbing his arm.

Miley grabbed Oliver's other arm. "No, tell her you're *my* friend."

"You tell her you were my friend first," Lilly said, pulling Oliver in one direction.

Miley yanked in the other direction. "You tell her to pick a new friend."

"Guys, could you please just work this out?" Oliver begged.

The girls yelled at him in unison. "Stay out of it!" Then they turned their backs to each other with a *hmph*. The next thing they heard was a click.

Oliver had handcuffed them together!

"What are you doing?" Miley demanded.

"Staying out of it," Oliver said.

"Very funny, Oliver. Now unlock these things," Lilly said.

But Oliver knew his life would be miserable until they made up. Miley would keep trying to turn him into Lilly, and Lilly would keep trying to steal him away from Miley. "No, not until you guys work this out," he insisted.

"Oliver, I have to be at the studio in two hours to do a live satellite feed!" Miley cried.

He hesitated, but he had to admit she had a point. "Fine," Oliver snapped. "But if it weren't for your stupid Booty, this totally would've worked." He started searching through his pockets. He reached into one, then the other, and then the first one again.

"Tell me you didn't lose the key," Miley said.

"I didn't lose the key," Oliver sputtered. But it was clear that he had.

"Oliver!" Miley screamed.

"Okay, I lost it," he admitted. "But Mom keeps a spare. I'll just jump on my bike, go home, and get it." He ran toward the bike rack . . . and saw that his ride had vanished! Apparently, some quick-thinking thief had taken advantage of the fact that he had unlocked his bike to use his handcuffs on Miley and Lilly.

"Someone stole my bike!" he yelled.

"Run!" Miley shouted, glaring at him.

"Fast!" Lilly ordered.

Oliver took off.

Miley watched him go. "We're doomed," she said.

"Why?" Lilly asked.

Miley pointed in the other direction, taking Lilly's arm with her. "His house is that way."

Chapter Five

A couple of hours later, Mr. Stewart came downstairs wearing his manager disguise. Jackson was wearing what seemed like a disguise of his own. He had a handkerchief wrapped around his head and an apron covering his clothes. He was busily mopping the kitchen floor.

"Hey, Dad!" Jackson said. "Remember two years ago when I spilled that soda and you told me to clean up and I totally ignored you?"

Mr. Stewart didn't say a word.

"Well, look who's mopping now. I did the dishes. And I cleaned the bathroom and my room, and I did the laundry and nothing's green, plus I made you a chocolate cake," Jackson said, barely pausing to take a breath.

His father walked around the kitchen, checking Jackson's work. Everything looked spotless.

"I promise I'll do whatever you ask, first time you ask. Second, tops!" Jackson continued frantically. "'Cause I'm still just a kid, but a kid who misses the sound of his daddy's voice! Please," he begged. Then he pointed to the chocolate cake. "It's got pudding in the middle!"

"Chocolate or vanilla?" Mr. Stewart asked with a smile.

"Actually, it's pistachio—ooooh, you

talked to me! You finally talked to me," Jackson said, throwing his arms around his father.

"That's because even though I didn't say anything, you finally heard me," Mr. Stewart explained.

"Yeah, I did," Jackson agreed. "Loud and clear."

"Jackson, that's all a parent ever wants. That and grandkids."

Jackson cringed and pulled back. "Now?" he asked, horrified.

"Don't worry," Mr. Stewart said, patting him on the back. "No rush on that one."

Miley paced back and forth, growing more and more frustrated as the minutes ticked by. Lilly had her own frustrations. She was sitting in a chair trying to eat an apple, and Miley's handcuffed arm kept jerking her hand and her apple just out of reach.

"What is taking Oliver so long?" Miley said impatiently.

"What do you expect? It's Oliver," Lilly said. "Now would you stop pacing?"

"You stop sitting," Miley retorted.

"No!" Lilly said stubbornly.

"Fine!" Miley said, just as stubbornly. She hadn't forgotten that she was mad at Lilly. Miley kept pacing. Suddenly, her cell phone rang. As she reached to answer it, she yanked Lilly's arm, and the apple fell to the ground.

Lilly looked down. "Aw, man! You owe me an apple."

"Would you keep it down? I'm on the phone," Miley snapped. "Hey, Oliver, where are you?" she said into the phone. "Oh, great. Just meet us down at the studio." Miley hung up and started to walk toward her house.

Lilly dug her heels in, forcing Miley to stop short.

"Come on," Miley urged. "Oliver's got to go down to the police station and get the key from his mom. And I've got to get ready." She tried to leave again.

Lilly yanked her back. "Not until you buy me another apple," she said.

"Forget about the apple!" Miley shouted. Then she lowered her voice. "Help me get ready and you can keep any three Hannah outfits you want."

Lilly considered this. "What about shoes?"

"One pair," Miley said.

"Two," Lilly countered.

"Nothing Italian," Miley warned.

"Fine," Lilly agreed.

The girls made it to Miley's secret Hannah Montana closet without incident, but transforming Miley into Hannah while she was still handcuffed to Lilly was another matter. Miley tried to get out of her hoodie, but somehow Lilly ended up wearing half of it. And Lilly's T-shirt was stretched across both of their bodies.

"Okay. This may be harder than we thought," Lilly said.

"Okay, let's go change," Miley said. She took a step onto the carousel in the closet that held her Hannah clothes, but Lilly walked in the other direction. The next thing they knew, both girls hit the floor with a thud.

The carousel started to turn. Somehow, Lilly ended up on her back with her legs coming out of the neck hole of Miley's T-shirt. Her feet were on either side of Miley's head.

"Okay, this is definitely not an improvement," Lilly said.

"Ewww! Your feet stink!" Miley cried.

"Yeah? How do you like them now?" Lilly asked, moving her feet closer to Miley's nose.

The carousel kept turning, but the girls managed to sit upright. Miley found an outfit she thought the two of them could get into. "It's a little tight, but I think it may work," she said. "Let's take a look in the mirror." She leaned over and picked Lilly up. The girls were back-to-back—both of them squeezed into the same dress.

Miley leaned over, and Lilly got a look at her upside-down self in the mirror. "Oooh, lovely," she said. Then she sneezed.

Rip!

The girls looked at the ruined dress, then hopped back into the closet.

* * *

An hour later, still handcuffed, Miley and Lilly walked into the television studio as Hannah and Lola.

Mr. Stewart was already there. "Aw, look at that," he said when the girls arrived. "I knew you two couldn't stay mad at each other."

"Oh, yeah. We're closer than ever." Miley lifted her arm to reveal the handcuffs holding her and Lilly together.

"You wanna tell me how this happened?" her father asked.

"Well, Oliver thought that—"

"Oh, sweet niblets," said Mr. Stewart. "I wish that boy would stop doing that."

Miley plastered a fake smile on her face so the stagehands wouldn't know anything was wrong and said to Lilly, "This never would have happened if you had just picked me."

"I'm not the one who gave a limo ride to a plant," Lilly said with an equally big smile.

"At least if Fern were playing flag football, she would have just picked me," Miley said through clenched teeth.

"It's a ficus!" Lilly cried, raising her voice.

"Named Fern!" Miley insisted.

"You could not pay me enough money to be a teenage girl," Mr. Stewart said, shaking his head.

Oliver rushed in. "I've got the key! I've got the key," he said breathlessly.

A stage manager listened to what was coming through his headset. "You're live in one minute, Miss Montana," he said.

Oliver struggled to get the key into the lock.

"Get her done, son," Mr. Stewart told him. "Carrie Underwood's on a stage in

Nashville announcing Hannah's won the award right now."

"Oh, man," Miley said nervously. "I haven't even thought of what I'm going to say yet!"

"Lucky for you, I did. All you've got to do is read the teleprompter. Your daddy's thought of everything," Mr. Stewart told her.

Oliver got the key into the lock and twisted. The next thing they knew, half of the key had broken off and fallen to the floor. The other half was still stuck inside the handcuffs.

"Except the key breaking," Mr. Stewart added.

"Uh-oh," Oliver said. He knew those handcuffs were not coming off, at least not without a locksmith.

Miley looked at her father. "I hate it when he says 'uh-oh.'"

"It's almost as bad as when he thinks," Mr. Stewart said.

The stage manager rushed past. "Live in thirty seconds."

"Oh, boy," Miley said. She was freaked!

Lilly was enjoying Miley's predicament. After all, the other night Lilly had to wait an hour for a ride because Miley drove home a plant instead of her. "Gee, I wonder what's going to happen now?" she said with a huge smile.

Miley imitated her. *"Gee, I wonder what's gonna happen now?"*

"I have an idea!" Oliver exclaimed.

Miley, Lilly, and Mr. Stewart all reacted the same way. "Nooooo!" they shouted.

But Oliver wasn't giving up. "Normally I'd agree," he said. "But this is a good one."

Chapter Six

Seconds later, Miley heard her cue. "Accepting her award live from Los Angeles, Hannah Montana," said the announcer. The red light on the camera went on.

Miley sat in a director's chair in front of the stage curtain, still dressed as Hannah. Her hands were clasped in front of her. Her silver Booty was on a table next to her. "Thank you so much for this incredible honor," she said, smiling into the camera.

"And it means even more knowing that it's coming from all the good folks in Nashville. . . ."

Miley's right hand seemed to have a mind of its own. It started to rise. Her fingers flapped next to her mouth, as if to say "blah, blah, blah." The viewers couldn't tell that it was really Lilly's hand.

Miley grabbed Lilly's right hand with her left and tried to pull it back down. Had anyone noticed that she was wearing black nail polish on one hand and buff on the other? ". . . the place I'm proud to call my hometown," she went on, struggling to keep Lilly's hand in check.

But Lilly, who was crouched behind Miley out of sight, had other ideas. Her arm was stronger than Miley's, too. Lilly raised their clasped hands up into the air and shook them in victory.

"Hooray, Nashville," Miley said, covering. She jerked their hands back down, accidentally hitting herself in the stomach. "I only wish I could be there in person to show you how I truly feel."

Lilly pulled her hand away, then put her thumb in Miley's ear and waggled her fingers.

Miley looked at the hand, horrified. "Uh, this is my special wave to Grandma," she said. She put her own thumb in the other ear and waggled her fingers. She could just imagine the headlines: HANNAH MONTANA IMITATES A MOOSE ON NATIONAL TELEVISION! "Hi, Grandma! Bye, Grandma!" she said, grabbing Lilly's hand again and bringing it down to her lap.

Behind the curtain, Lilly rolled her eyes. Miley wasn't getting off that easy.

Miley continued reading from the

teleprompter: "Every time I hear 'True Friend' it always makes me think . . ."

Lilly put her hand on Miley's chin in a fake "thoughtful" pose.

Miley tried to continue, even though Lilly started moving Miley's head back and forth. ". . . about real friendship and—"

Lilly's finger suddenly hooked Miley's mouth, stretching it like a fishhook would.

"Aaaah!" Miley screamed. She grabbed Lilly's hand. "Sorry," she said into the camera. "I had a little something in my teeth." Miley used Lilly's fingers to rub her teeth. "All better."

Lilly cringed. She hadn't counted on her fingers being used as a toothbrush.

This situation was getting worse by the second, but Miley was a true professional. She kept her eyes on the teleprompter and the speech her father had written for her.

"As I was saying," she continued, acting as if she hadn't just been completely and totally mortified on national TV, "friendship means a lot to me. In fact, this song was inspired by my . . ." Miley paused. She shot her father a look.

Mr. Stewart nodded.

Clearly, he was trying to get her and Lilly back together, Miley thought. Well, it wasn't going to work. Miley was too mad.

". . . my best friend," Miley said grudgingly. "She's been with me through everything. And even though we sometimes fight, we know we'll always get through it . . . because we love each other," Miley finished, stroking Lilly's arm with her free hand.

Smiling to herself, Lilly rested her head on Miley's back with a small smile.

"Nothing says it better than the song,"

Miley said. She began to quote the lyrics. Suddenly Lilly sneezed.

"Bless you," Miley said automatically.

Lilly's hand came up again and gently patted Miley's chest. Miley patted Lilly's hand with her own.

"Thank you for believing in me, and thank you for this award. I love you all," Miley said into the camera. "Bye."

Lilly's hand came up and started waving good-bye.

Miley waved her hand as well. Now her smile was real. "Good night!"

Mr. Stewart and Oliver nodded to each other with satisfaction.

As soon as the camera's red light switched off, Miley pulled Lilly out from her hiding place. "I'm sorry!" she said, blinking away her tears.

"Me, too!" Lilly replied tearfully.

They tried to hug, but each time their arms ended up at an uncomfortable angle.

Then they found the perfect position, side to side, cheek to cheek. *"Awww,"* they said together.

The next day at school, the girls lined up for flag football. Miley and Lilly stood next to each other. There were two new captains.

"Let's go, ladies. Pick your teams," Mrs. McDermott ordered. "You move slower than my husband in the bathroom."

"You said that last week," Miley told her.

"I know. Now he's got a minifridge in there."

A plasma screen *and* a minifridge? Miley and Lilly glanced at each other.

"I think he's hiding from me," Mrs. McDermott added, heading for the other side of the field.

"I could never imagine why," Miley said under her breath.

Lilly snorted.

One of the captains chose her first player. "Okay, I pick Joannie," she said.

The girls snickered as Joannie walked by. Half her head was shaved bald. Lilly felt a little bad, but a bet's a bet.

Joannie leaned in and glared at Lilly.

"Hey, you could have bet a quarter," Lilly pointed out to her.

Now it was the second captain's turn to choose. "I pick Lilly."

"If you pick me, you've got to pick Miley, too," Lilly said.

"But I don't want to pick her," the second captain complained.

"I don't care. Wherever I go, she goes," Lilly said.

"Yeah, we're kind of a package deal."

Miley lifted her arm to show that they were still handcuffed together.

The captain made no attempt to hide her disgust. "Fine. I'll take Lilly and Stinky."

"I told you it would work," Lilly said to Miley. "Now unlock us."

Miley's face fell. "I thought you had the key."

"Aw, man," Lilly said, rolling her eyes.

"Think fast!" Mrs. McDermott yelled, throwing a football in their direction.

The two friends caught it together.

Part One

"How about winning captain gets to give losing captain . . . a little haircut?" Miley suggested.

"Who's Fern?" Lilly, dressed as Lola, asked as Hannah started to leave.

"Oh, come on! Come *on*!" Jackson pleaded.

"Guys, could you please just work this out?" Oliver begged.

"I promise I'll do whatever you ask, first time you ask. Second, tops!" Jackson told his dad.

"Okay," Lilly said. "This may be harder than we thought."

Smiling to herself, Lilly rested her head on Hannah's back.

"Thank you for believing in me," Hannah said, "and thank you for this award."

Part Two

"Yeah! Yeah! Yeah!" Hannah chanted, pumping her arms in the air.

"You don't want to be late for your first day of high school," Mr. Stewart said. "Don't make me get the water bucket."

"Somebody knows I'm Hannah Montana!" Miley said, panicked.

"Sorry," Miley told Rico. "I just got lost in your eyes, your beady little eyes."

"I am never coming home for lunch again," Jackson said when he saw his dad singing to himself.

"Who wants to trade a silly little phone for a nice banana?" Lilly asked the monkey in Rico's locker.

"Get your stinkin' paws off me, you darn, dirty ape!" Oliver shouted.

Shocked, Miley pulled back, sputtering. "He's toast!" she cried.

PART TWO

Chapter One

Miley Stewart was onstage, dressed as her alter ego, pop-music star Hannah Montana. She brought her sold-out concert to a close with the final chorus of her hit song "Make Some Noise." The crowd cheered. They loved Hannah Montana and her music. Miley did, too, but she also wanted to live the life of a regular teenager. Only a few people knew high school freshman Miley Stewart and teen superstar

Hannah Montana were the same person.

"Everyone who's starting a new school year on Monday, let me hear y'all make some noise!" Miley called into the microphone.

The audience burst into a chorus of unhappy boos.

Miley laughed. "Aw, come on. Wrong noise, wrong noise," she said. "We all have to do it. So we might as well have fun. How about we all jump out of bed on Monday and say, 'Yeah!' Let me hear ya say it! Yeah! Yeah! Yeah!" she chanted, pumping her arms in the air and urging them on.

The crowed roared, chanting along with her. "Yeah! Yeah! Yeah!"

By Monday morning, Miley felt a little differently about school. She was deep under the covers, holding her stuffed bear. Her father shook her gently.

"No. No. No," she moaned.

"Come on, Miley," Robby Stewart said. "Just jump out of bed and say, 'Yeah! Yeah! Yeah! Yeah!'"

Miley wasn't exactly thrilled that he was throwing her own words in her face—especially this early in the morning. Without opening her eyes, she reached out and patted her father's face until she found his nose. Then she pressed it.

"What are you doing?" he asked.

"Looking for the snooze button," she replied. Then she rolled over and pulled the covers over her head. It couldn't be the first day of school already. It seemed as if summer vacation had started about five minutes ago.

"Oh, no," her father said. "You don't

want to be late for your first day of high school."

Miley groaned, but she didn't budge. She was excited about the idea of starting high school—just not this early in the morning.

"Don't make me get the water bucket," Mr. Stewart threatened.

Miley gasped and popped her head out from under the covers. "You wouldn't."

Her older brother, Jackson, ran in from the hall, shivering and soaking wet. "Oh, yes, he would," he told her.

That was enough for Miley. A hot shower was a better way to start the day than a cold bucket of water. She threw the covers off and jumped out of bed.

An hour later, Miley and her best friend, Lilly Truscott, stood in the school's courtyard, also known as the quad. The quad served as a between-class hangout and outdoor cafeteria. The girls had realized it was also ideal for people watching. A couple of cute boys walked past, and suddenly Miley didn't mind having to get out of bed so early. "Junior boys," she said to Lilly. Then she spotted someone even cuter. "Senior boys," she added.

"Can you believe it?" Lilly asked excitedly. "Yesterday we were girls."

"Today we are . . . high school girls," Miley said, finishing for her.

Now it was time for a very important ritual. A before-school body check. Miley and Lilly moved to a spot where no one would see them. "Breath," they said together, then exhaled in each other's faces.

Breath check over, they moved on.

"Pits," Lilly said. They raised their arms and took a sniff.

"Boogies," Miley said. She threw back her head and flared her nostrils as Lilly did the same.

"Zits," they said at the same time, peering at each other's faces.

"You're good," Lilly told Miley.

"You're . . ." Miley said, moving in for a closer look. She was about to give Lilly the all clear, but then she noticed an ugly red pimple right between her friend's eyebrows. "Yeow! Why don't we just move the hat down?" She pulled Lilly's pink knit cap so low it covered her eyes.

Just then, Jackson crossed the quad. "Hey, bro," Miley said.

Jackson stopped. He pointed to himself. "Junior," he said. Then he pointed to Miley. "Freshman. No 'bro.' Gotta go."

Miley rolled her eyes. Jackson had been warning her all summer not to ruin his high school rep. As if her dorky brother would be damaged by having a sister, Miley thought.

Lilly grabbed her friend's arm. "Miley, I can't walk around like this all day. I look like a sock puppet. Do you have any cover-up?"

The two friends walked to a picnic table and sat down. Lilly started looking through Miley's backpack for a makeup case. Instead, she found Miley's stuffed bear.

"You brought Barry Bear?" Lilly asked in disbelief. How uncool was that? Being seen with a stuffed animal on the first day of high school was the kind of thing that could follow Miley through all four years. Plus it would make Lilly look totally uncool just by association.

"Put him back! I don't want anyone to see him," Miley whispered.

Lilly shoved the bear into the backpack. "Then why'd you bring him?"

"Because," Miley said defensively, "it's a big day and I'm nervous. . . ." Suddenly Miley got sheepish. "He wanted to see the school," she added.

"Yeah. Okay," Lilly said sarcastically. "Well, he's seen it. Now, would you zip him back up, please?"

"Fine. But not all the way. He's afraid of the dark." Miley gave Barry Bear a quick kiss before zipping up her backpack.

"Do you realize what would happen to your rep if people saw you with that bear?" Lilly asked. "I can't imagine a more horrible first day of high school."

While she was listening, Miley got a text message on her cell phone. Her eyes widened. "I can," she said, scared. She handed Lilly the phone. "Look at this text."

"'I know your secret,'" Lilly read aloud.

Nobody at school knew that Miley Stewart and Hannah Montana were the same girl. And that's the way Miley wanted to keep it. She had realized long ago that if the kids at school found out she was the hottest teen pop singer in the country, she could never have a normal life.

She had the best of both worlds. She was regular old Miley Stewart until she put on a long blonde wig and glittery outfits and became Hannah Montana. The only people in the whole world who knew the truth were Miley's family and her friends Lilly and Oliver.

The only people until now, Miley thought. Her secret was out. "Somebody knows I'm Hannah Montana!" Miley said, panicked.

Chapter Two

Miley was completely freaked out. "What am I gonna do?" she asked. "I've tried so hard to keep the secret. This is going to ruin everything."

"You don't know that," Lilly said rationally. "So one other person knows. It doesn't mean they're going to tell everybody at lunch."

Miley's phone buzzed again, letting her know another message had arrived. "Oh, no, I'm getting another text!" she cried.

"What does it say?" Lilly asked. She peered over her friend's shoulder.

"'I'm going to tell everybody at lunch,'" Miley read.

"Wow, creepy," Lilly said. She took the phone and read the rest of the message. "What's 'mwah-ah-ah-ah'?" she asked.

"I think it's more like . . ." Miley rubbed her hands together, threw her head back, and laughed evilly. "Mwah-ah-ah-ah!"

Then she got serious. "In two hours, any chance I have of being a normal high school girl is over!" she cried.

"Tell me about it," said Lilly. "If people find out you're . . ." she leaned in and whispered, ". . . Anna-hay Ontana-may, you won't be able to go to any school! Except maybe in the South Pole, completely cut off from civilization, where you'll eventually go mad." Lilly's voice rose. "Mad, I tell you. *Mad!*"

Miley leaned back and studied her friend. That was over the top even for Lilly. "You put extra sugar on your cereal this morning, didn't you?" Miley asked.

"Yes," Lilly admitted. Then she put her hands to her head. "And now the room is spinning!"

On the other side of campus, Jackson walked down a school hallway toward his locker. A stocky guy wearing overalls stashed books in the next locker. He greeted Jackson with a huge smile. "Hello."

"Hey," Jackson answered absently. He was in a hurry to catch up with his friends. He opened his locker and put a couple of books away. When he closed it, the big guy was still there.

"Hello," the guy said again, just as cheerfully.

"Hey, again." Jackson started to walk away, but the guy followed closely. When Jackson stopped, the big guy stopped. When Jackson moved to the right, the other guy moved right. Could this really be happening? Jackson wondered. To be sure, he spun in a circle. Sure enough, so did the big guy.

"This is a hoot!" said the guy. "What are we doing, eh?"

"Who are you?" Jackson asked, confused.

"I'm Thor. The new guy, don'tcha know."

Thor's overalls and midwestern accent gave him away. Jackson knew a country bumpkin when he saw one, and he knew enough to stay away. Far, far away. "Okay, well, I'll see you at the twenty-fifth reunion," Jackson said, trying to escape.

But Thor grabbed the straps to Jackson's backpack and pulled him back. "Where are you going? Those guys said you're the welcoming committee." Thor pointed to a group of guys who tried not to crack up while they watched the action. They waved, and one of the guys gave Jackson a thumbs-up sign.

"Oh, I get it," Jackson said. "Those are my friends. They're just messing with you," he explained. "Real funny, guys!" he called to his friends.

"Ya, real mature," Thor agreed. "Make fun of the new guy! And the short one!" he added as he threw his arm around Jackson.

"Hey!" Jackson said, pulling away. He didn't like to be reminded that he was what he liked to call "vertically challenged." He made up for it with personality.

"Don't you worry," Thor said as he put his arm around Jackson again. "We don't need those hockey pucks."

"Good point," Jackson said, pretending to agree. Thor obviously wasn't going to take the hint and disappear on his own. Jackson had to resort to other means. "Hey, race ya to the fourth floor!" he exclaimed, taking a step toward the stairs.

That was all the encouragement Thor needed. "Okay!" he yelled. He took off and raced up the stairs.

Jackson stopped after one more step and headed back toward his buddies.

"Hey, man, we don't have a fourth floor," his friend Max pointed out.

Jackson knew that all along. He was just trying to get rid of Thor. Still, he shrugged and covered his mouth in mock surprise. "Oops!"

Miley and Lilly walked through the hall on their way to class. Miley was still staring at her cell phone. "I have got to figure out who this is," she said. "I didn't tell anyone, you didn't tell anyone—"

Miley cut herself off. Suddenly, everyone was a suspect, even her own best friend. "You didn't tell anyone, did you?" she asked threateningly.

"Of course not!" Lilly replied.

"Well, who else could it be?" Miley asked.

Just then, their friend Oliver Oken walked down the stairs. He was acting like a big man on campus. "Hey, what's up?" he said to kids who passed by. "How's it going?" he asked a pretty girl, puffing out his chest.

Miley and Lilly had seen Oliver's cool-guy act before, but today he didn't look like himself. He looked like a weight lifter. His muscles were huge! But as he got closer, the girls noticed that he was just wearing a supertight T-shirt over soft padding. He looked more like a life-size stuffed animal than a Mr. Universe.

Miley reached out and pulled Oliver toward her.

"Hey watch out there," he said.

"What did you do?" Miley asked.

"Nothing," Oliver said defensively. He puffed out his chest again and flexed his "muscles." "I've just been working out on the old bicep, tricep—"

"Oliver!" Lilly cried, cutting him off.

"Forget the muscles, meatball!" Miley shouted. She grabbed Oliver by the shirt and pulled him toward her again. They were nose to nose. "You told someone my secret, didn't you? Didn't you?"

"No, I swear!" Oliver raised his arms in surrender. "And go easy on the pecs." He looked around to see if anyone could hear. "They pop," he whispered.

Miley's phone jingled. "Oh, no, incoming," she said.

Oliver read over Miley's shoulder. "'Wondering what you can do to stop me? I have an idea.'" Then he turned toward Miley. "Who is this?"

"I don't know!" Miley said, exasperated. At least now she knew that it wasn't Oliver. But her normal high school life was about to end—before it had even started.

"I got it!" Lilly exclaimed. "All we have to do is look for the person texting."

The three friends looked around. There were lots of kids in the hallway, and all of them were busy sending text messages before their first class.

"That narrows it down," Miley said sarcastically. "Everybody!"

Lilly shrugged weakly. At least she had tried.

Chapter Three

In his first class, Jackson sat a lab table. He wore safety goggles and oven mitts. He was in the middle of explaining something to two of his classmates. "I love chemistry," he said. "It's educational." He sat back and pointed to the marshmallow he was roasting on the Bunsen burner. "And delicious!"

His teacher, Mrs. Carter, came up behind him. "Can I get you some chocolate and graham crackers to go with that?" she asked sweetly.

"Oh, yeah, that'd be—" The word "awesome" got stuck in his throat when Jackson realized who had asked the question. "—totally inappropriate, because I shouldn't even be doing this." He blew on the marshmallow and looked around him. "Okay people, everybody stop fooling around."

"Now lose the marshmallow, Stewart," Mrs. Carter said, all the sweetness gone from her voice.

"Yes, ma'am." Jackson turned off the Bunsen burner and put the marshmallow in his mouth. Then he gasped. "Hot! Hot! Hot!" he cried as he turned to the person who had just sat down on the other side of his lab table. "Really hot," Jackson added when he saw that it was an incredibly pretty girl.

"Hi. Is this seat taken?" she asked with a smile.

Jackson tried to be nonchalant. "No, go for it," he said. The minute her back was turned, he spit out his marshmallow and ditched the oven mitts and safety goggles. "I'm Jackson," he said, trying to sound cool.

"Hey, I'm Anne."

Thor suddenly popped his head between them. "And I'm Thor, his new best buddy," he said, leaning an elbow on Jackson's shoulder. "And I was kinda hoping I could sit there."

"No!" Jackson yelled. He signaled to Thor to beat it by pointing and gesturing with his head. At first, Thor didn't get it.

"Ohhhh, I get it!" Thor finally said in a loud voice. "You like her." Then he turned to Anne. "He likes you!"

Jackson was completely horrified.

"Look at his face!" Thor laughed. "He's redder than a cow's udder on a cold day."

Jackson didn't think things could get any worse, but then Thor went on about cow udders.

"Of course, they're pretty much always red, what with all the yanking, don'tcha know."

Jackson was speechless.

Anne picked up her books and started to edge away. "Maybe you two should sit together. And I'll sit . . ." She looked around. "Anywhere else."

Thor took the empty seat while Jackson sadly watched Anne walk away. "But . . . but I have marshmallows," Jackson sputtered.

Thor popped one in his mouth, oblivious to what had just happened. "Since she doesn't seem to be interested in you, do you mind if I take a shot?" He raised his hand for a high five.

Jackson didn't respond. He just started pounding his head on the table.

Slightly alarmed, Thor slid the soft bag of marshmallows over so it was between Jackson's forehead and the table. Then Thor smiled across the aisle at Anne, who looked stunned.

Miley, Lilly, and Oliver walked into their first class. They still wondered who had sent the mysterious text messages and what it would take to keep Miley's secret.

"I bet they want something," Lilly said. "Like money. Or concert tickets." Her eyes flashed with excitement as she thought about what she would want. "Oooh, if it were me, I'd take your wardrobe. And jewelry. And your shoes!" She closed her eyes and pictured Miley's secret Hannah Montana closet, filled with incredibly cool clothes and accessories. "Oh, yeah. Your shoes."

"Turn around. I'll give you one of my shoes right now," Miley warned, jolting Lilly back to the present.

"Sorry, I'm just trying to get into the mind of the criminal," Lilly said dramatically. "If you can understand them, you can catch them."

Miley dropped into a seat. "And then what, Sherlock? As long as they know my secret, I'll have to do whatever they want. What kind of monster would torture me like this?" she said with a moan.

Just then their teacher, Mrs. Espinosa, came into the room, cutting off any more conversation.

"Morning. Let's welcome a special young man to our class," she said. "He skipped a couple of grades, so he's a little younger."

She stepped aside, and the young man sauntered in with a cocky expression. "And a *lot* smarter," he added.

"This is Rico," Mrs. Espinosa said.

Miley's jaw dropped. Rico's father owned the surf shop on the beach where Jackson worked after school. Rico lived to play tricks on other people, and Jackson and Miley were two of his favorite targets.

He stopped at Miley's desk on his way to his seat. "Hiya toots, get my messages?" he asked with a wink.

Miley and Lilly eyed each other with dread. If Rico knew Miley's secret, then she was in trouble—serious trouble.

Chapter Four

At the end of class, Lilly smiled sweetly at the teacher. "Don't worry, Mrs. Espinosa. We'll take good care of the new kid."

She and Oliver each grabbed an arm and carried Rico across the hall. They dropped him against a locker. Miley faced him. The three friends were each at least a foot and a half taller than Rico, but he eyed them with total confidence.

"All right, short stack, how'd you find out?" Miley demanded.

"Simple," Rico answered with a cocky smile. "You were careless, and I had a camera phone." Then he threw his head back and demonstrated his evil laugh. "Mwah-ah-ah-ah!"

Miley and her friends didn't laugh. "Give me that phone, or you will never make it to four feet," Miley threatened.

"Feel free to pat me down, kitten," Rico teased. "But it's safe." He pointed behind him. "In my locker."

Rico didn't know that opening lockers for kids who had forgotten their combinations was one of Oliver's special talents. In middle school, it had even earned him a nickname. "Step aside, squirt," Oliver said, "and let the Locker Doctor operate."

Rico stepped aside with a smirk. Oliver blew on his fingertips and got ready to work his magic. He quickly beat on the locker with the side of his fist and the door popped open.

"Oh, yeah!" Oliver said, pumping his fist in the air. He reached in and pulled out a huge football jersey. "Wow, that's a really big jersey for such a little—"

"I didn't say it was my locker," Rico said with a satisfied smile.

Oliver turned around to find himself face-to-chest with a football player—a huge football player.

"Hey, fresh meat," the player said with a growl. "What are you doing crammed inside my locker?"

"I'm not crammed inside your—" Suddenly Oliver realized that that was exactly what the football player intended to do to him. Oliver's voice rose two octaves. "My mom's a cop!" he squealed. He threw the jersey in the player's face, then took off down the hall. The football player was right on his heels.

Miley hoped Oliver could run faster than the big guy, but her main problem was still standing in front of her. "Okay, Rico. You know the secret. What's it gonna take to shut you up?" she asked.

"You. As my girlfriend," Rico replied.

Miley's jaw dropped in disbelief. Did Rico have a crush on her? "Say what?"

"Don't flatter yourself, doll face, this is strictly business," he explained. "I need some hall cred in this place, and you can help me get it."

"Ohhh, so all he's looking for is a little arm candy," Lilly said to Miley.

Rico nodded. "That, and someone to reach the top shelf of my locker."

"You can totally do that!" Lilly said with a laugh.

Miley pretended to laugh and told Lilly to be quiet.

"Of course, if you'd rather I send your picture to everyone at school . . ." Rico threatened.

"Miley, you have to do what he says. It's either that or your secret's out," Lilly said.

Miley plastered a big, fake smile on her face. "So far, high school stinks!"

That day at lunch in the quad, Rico sat on a picnic table. Miley sat on the bench below him, making them almost the same height. They were surrounded by ninth graders.

"I remember how I met my woman," Rico declared. He put his arm around Miley and yanked her toward him. "I had just come out of the ocean, my skin shining like . . ." he turned to Miley. "What was it shining like, love monkey?"

Miley knew what she was supposed to say. Rico had given her a list to memorize. "A new penny in the piggy bank of my heart," she answered without a trace of enthusiasm.

"What can I say?" Rico said. "She's crazy in love." He picked up a cracker and turned toward Miley. "Cheese me," he demanded, putting the cracker between his lips.

Miley gritted her teeth and picked up a can of cheese spread. She sprayed it on the cracker, then all over Rico's upper lip.

"Enough!" Rico shouted, furious.

"Sorry, I just got lost in your eyes," Miley said. Then she leaned in and whispered, "Your beady little eyes."

"Secrets," he warned quietly.

"Right," Miley said. "Please forgive me."

Rico nodded his forgiveness. "Now go get daddy a moist towelette." Rico threw his arm over his head and snapped his fingers like a bullfighter.

If Miley weren't so humiliated, she actually might have laughed. Rico still had cheese hanging from his nose. Miley swallowed her real reply. "Of course," she said.

Miley walked into school in search of a bathroom and a paper towel. She wondered how bad it would be if Rico revealed her secret.

Miley thought about what her dad had said and mimicked his voice. *"You know, bud, you can always be homeschooled."* Then Miley repeated her answer. *"No, Daddy, I want to go to school like a normal kid."* She shook her head at the memory. "What was I thinking?" she said aloud.

Lilly rushed down the stairs. "There you are! I've got great news!"

"Unless it involves a time machine and

Rico's parents never meeting, I don't want to know," Miley said.

"Fine," Lilly replied. "I won't tell you Oliver found Rico's locker."

"Good," Miley said distractedly. She was too focused on her own problems to really listen. "'Cause we have to find Rico's—" Miley realized that was exactly what Lilly had just told her. "I'm going to stop talking now and follow you."

"That would be nice," Lilly said.

Together, they ran up the stairs.

Chapter Five

Jackson had his own problems. Every time he turned around, Thor was there. Jackson had had to climb out a window overlooking the parking lot to escape. Then he'd headed home for lunch. He couldn't handle Thor and cafeteria food at the same time.

Mr. Stewart was in the middle of the living room, still wearing his pajamas and bathrobe. After a summer full of Jackson and Miley, not to mention a Hannah Montana tour, he was happy to finally have the house all to himself. He picked up a guitar and started strumming a sad tune.

"My kids are gone, so I'm writin' this song," he sang. *"And you think it's so sad—"*

Then he climbed up on the coffee table and picked up the pace. *"But you're oh so wrong. I can pick my nose, and nobody stares; I can dance around in my underwear. Ah, yeah!"*

Having just walked through the door, Jackson couldn't believe it. Is this what his father did when he and Miley were at school? "I am never coming home for lunch again," Jackson said.

"Good, because this is my Robby Ray time!" Mr. Stewart answered. He climbed down from the table.

"I didn't plan on coming home," Jackson

explained. He collapsed into a chair. "I just couldn't take it anymore."

"Take what?" Mr. Stewart asked.

"Okay, some guy from *Moooo*-ville, Minnesota, decided I'm his new best buddy, and now he won't leave me alone. If I have to hear that stupid accent one more time, I'm gonna beat myself unconscious with—*a frozen trout, don'tcha know*." He said the last part of the sentence mimicking Thor's accent and upbeat tone.

"I seem to remember another new kid with a funny accent a few years ago," Mr. Stewart said. "Let's see, what was his name? Paxon? Saxon?"

Jackson shuddered, remembering. On his first day in Malibu, he had walked into school dressed in his coolest Tennessee clothes. A big, red cowboy hat, a colorful, embroidered rodeo shirt, and red-and-blue cowboy boots. "Howdy y'all!" he had said to the first group of guys he saw. "I'm Jackson."

"I didn't know there was a rodeo in town," one of them had answered with a laugh.

"There's a rodeo in town? Eeeee doggies!" Jackson had cried.

"He was talking about your getup," another guy explained.

"You like it?" Jackson asked proudly. "Then check this out!" He pushed a button on his belt and the enormous buckle lit up and started to flash. "Back home in Tennessee, that's what we call *blang*."

"It's bling," said the first guy.

"That's what I said, *blang*!" Jackson repeated.

"What a loser," said one of the guys.

Jackson covered up his belt while the

other guys laughed. The last thing he heard as he slunk away was an insult.

"Ride 'em, cowboy!"

Jackson cringed at the memory.

Mr. Stewart continued to recite names that sounded like Jackson. "Crackson, Shellackson—"

"Enough, Dad!" Jackson cried. "I already had the flashback."

"What I'm saying, son, is think about what happened to you," Mr. Stewart said. "You might want to cut this boy some slack."

"Why is this my problem?" Jackson asked. "Nobody cut me a break. If I had to tough it out, then so can he. And that's exactly what I'm going to tell him."

"Jackson, don't you think it'd be better if—"

"Good day," Jackson said, cutting his

father off. He headed toward the door. He had forgotten all about lunch. The last thing he needed was someone ruining his social life as a high school junior. And his father wasn't going to make him feel guilty about that.

"Son, I—"

"I said, 'good day,' Daddy!" Jackson stormed out the door.

Mr. Stewart watched him leave and then started to play his guitar again. *"Now Jackson is gone,"* he sang. *"And I am so happy. I think I'll go upstairs and take me a nappy."* He finished with some hot guitar licks and yelled, "Good night, Malibu!"

Meanwhile, Miley and Lilly rushed up the stairs to Rico's locker. Oliver stood in the hall, waiting for them.

"Oliver, how'd you find it?" Miley asked.

Someone had popped Oliver's "muscles," and he was back to his normal body, but he still puffed out his chest proudly. "Cunning, determination — " he started.

Lilly pushed him aside and pointed. "It was the only locker with a footstool in front of it," she explained, pointing to a small bench. Rico was the only kid in high school short enough to need one.

Oliver suddenly looked deflated. "Would it have killed you to let me have this one?" he asked.

"Guys, please!" Miley cried. She didn't have time for a Lilly and Oliver spat. She needed to get that camera phone and delete all evidence of her secret. "Sometime before Rico and I honeymoon in Hobbit Town!"

"Step aside, ladies," Oliver said. "The doctor is in." He drummed on the locker, then tapped it with his elbow. The door popped open, and he peered inside.

Rico's locker wasn't filled with the textbooks, notebooks, and posters of a typical student.

"What's with all the plants?" Oliver asked curiously. "And the waterfall? It's like a rain forest in there."

"Who cares? Can you see the phone?" Miley asked.

Lilly looked inside, her forehead wrinkled in confusion. How did Rico get a tropical rain forest into his locker? Then she spotted the phone. "Yeah. It's right there next to that—*monkey*!" Lilly yelled.

The three of them jumped back as the monkey howled and reached out to grab them.

Chapter Six

Jackson returned to school determined to tell Thor to back off. Jackson wasn't the welcoming committee, and he wasn't Thor's friend. Thor would have to find his own way in Malibu, just like Jackson had.

He saw a group of kids laughing on the quad. They were all crowded around the window to the science lab.

"Hey, Max," Jackson said, spotting one of his friends. "Have you seen Thor?"

"Yeah, he's in there," Max said, cracking up. "I told him California girls love guys who can churn their own butter."

Jackson looked through the window. Thor was covered in sweat, pumping the handle of a wooden butter churn up and down. The girls around him were laughing. Thor clearly thought they were laughing with him, but they weren't—they were laughing at him.

"Hey, butta-butta-butta," Thor chanted with a huge smile on his face. "Hey, butta-butta-butta."

"Churn!" everyone shouted together.

"Hey, butta-butta-butta," Thor continued.

"Churn!" the crowd shouted again.

"Oh, man," Jackson said. His heart sank. His dad might not have been able to guilt him into helping Thor, but his friends had. Thor was being totally and completely humiliated, and he didn't even know it!

Max shoved Jackson aside for a better view. "I know. This kid's dorkier than that light-up cowboy from freshman year. Remember?" he asked.

Jackson glared at him.

"Oh, wait, that was you," Max said, laughing even harder.

Thor was still chanting when Jackson entered the science lab.

"Okay, show's over," Jackson said to the crowd of students. "Knock it off."

"I can't, little buddy," Thor said. "I'm in the zone. Hey, butta-butta-butta."

"Not you!" Jackson yelled. He turned to the crowd, noticing that Anne was one of them. "You! And you. And you," he said, pointing. "All of you guys. Cut the dude a break! It doesn't make you cool to make fun of somebody, it just makes you all jerks."

Thor gave Jackson a confused look.

"All Thor wants to do is make some friends," Jackson said.

"And butter!" Thor exclaimed, smiling.

"You're not helping," Jackson told him through clenched teeth. "Now if you hockey pucks will excuse us, me and my new best buddy have some butter to churn."

"Okeydokey, artichokey," Thor said, handing over the butter churn.

Jackson started churning at warp speed. He just wanted to get this thing over with. "Hey, butta-butta-butta. Hey, butta-butta-butta. Hey, butta-butta-butta, churn!"

"Ooh, slow down there, buddy!" Thor warned. "You don't want to hit an air—"

At that moment, Jackson hit an air bubble. The butter exploded, covering him with the creamy mixture.

"—bubble," Thor finished.

"Sweet niblets," Jackson said, using one of the old Tennessee expressions that used to get him laughed at. "I've got butter in all my nooks and crannies."

Rico's monkey relentlessly teased Miley and her friends. It seemed to know exactly what they were after. The monkey held the phone out to Oliver and pulled it back in when he tried to grab it.

"Okay, I'll go stall Rico," Miley said. "Oliver, make friends with the monkey," she ordered.

Oliver watched her walk away. "And exactly how do I do that?" he asked Lilly.

"Just be yourself," Lilly said. "He'll think you're family."

Oliver stared at her. Since when was she so mean? "High school's made you hard."

"Coconut!" Lilly yelled.

"What kind of comeback is coco—" Oliver started to ask. But it wasn't a comeback; it was a warning. The monkey threw a coconut at the middle of Oliver's back.

Meanwhile, Miley raced down the stairs, catching Rico on the way up to his locker. She put a hand on his head and pushed him back. "Rico, honey, where are you going?"

"I gotta grab some books out of my locker," he said, trying to move past her.

Miley pushed him back another step.

Rico gave her a sly grin. "But save the 'honey' thing for later. Daddy likey." He snapped his fingers and moved past her.

Miley had to keep Rico away from his locker. She picked him up and sat him on a recycling bin. "You can't leave me!" she cried desperately.

Rico looked around. "You can cut the act, string bean. Nobody's watching."

"It's not an act," Miley said.

Rico eyed her with mistrust.

"Look, Rico, I know I said I couldn't stand you. But the truth is, deep down . . ." Miley struggled to come up with the words without gagging. ". . . way, way deep down," she added through clenched teeth, "I've always thought you were a hu—" The word got caught in Miley's throat. She tried again. "A hu—" And again. "A hu—" Finally, she forced the word out. "A hunk."

"Really?" Rico asked. His tone made it clear he still wasn't buying it.

"May I be hit by lightning if I'm lying," Miley said. She sneaked a peek out the window and stepped aside slightly, just in case.

* * *

Upstairs, Lilly and Oliver were still trying to get Rico's monkey to part with the cell phone.

Lilly waved a banana in front of the locker. "Who wants to trade a silly little phone for a nice banana," she said in a singsong voice.

Oliver grabbed the banana from her. "Why would he want a stupid banana?" he asked, using it to point into the locker. "He's got a snow-cone machine and a minifridge in—"

But maybe the monkey did want the banana. He grabbed Oliver's arm and tried to pull him into the locker.

"—theeeeeere!" Oliver screamed.

Lilly grabbed the back of his shirt, frantically trying to keep Oliver from getting yanked inside.

Chapter Seven

Downstairs, Miley was sitting at a picnic table on the quad with Rico in her lap.

"This feels so right, and yet something haunts me," Rico said, putting his arm around Miley. "How can I be sure your love is true?"

Miley rolled her eyes. "You're on my lap, aren't ya?"

Rico sighed. "Perhaps you could prove your love with a kiss."

"Oooookay," Miley said, checking the stairs. Where were Oliver and Lilly with that phone? "Who do you want me to kiss?" she asked, feigning ignorance.

Rico raised his eyebrows in a threatening way. She sighed.

"Okay, fine, I'll do it." She eyed the stairs again, hoping to see her friends running toward her with Rico's phone.

The stairs were empty.

"Let me just . . . ready myself," Miley said, stalling for time. She turned her back on Rico and started rummaging through her backpack, looking for lip gloss. "You know, this may . . . this *will* take some time."

Oliver was still half in and half out of Rico's locker. His feet were braced against the sides of the locker, but the monkey had a tight grip on Oliver's arms. If he lost his footing, he'd end up as Monkey Victim Number One. "Get your stinkin' paws off me, you darn, dirty ape!" he shouted.

Lilly had a tight grip on Oliver's shirt, but she couldn't hold on much longer. Oliver didn't seem to be helping at all. "C'mon, use your muscles!" she urged.

Oliver was totally frustrated. What did Lilly think he was doing? And besides those muscles weren't even real. "They're in my book bag!" he yelled.

Miley was still getting ready for her kiss. She was gargling . . . and gargling . . . and gargling. She had been gargling for so long that other kids were starting to notice.

"Hello, my lips are chappin', let's get smackin'!" Rico exclaimed.

Miley choked on her gargle water and was forced to swallow it. She eyed the stairs again. They were still empty! There was nothing left to do. She puckered up for the kiss, cringing.

Rico leaned in. Miley closed her eyes and whimpered.

"We got it!" Lilly yelled, running onto the quad.

"We got the phone!" Oliver shouted.

Just in time, Miley grabbed a chicken leg off someone's lunch tray and held it in front of Rico's lips. "Kiss the chicken, bub!" Miley said. Then she threw her head back and imitated Rico's evil laugh. "Mwah-ah-ah-ah!"

"Your little blackmail scheme is over," Oliver added. He opened the phone, ready to delete the incriminating photo. The phone squirted water right into his face.

Lilly and Miley gasped.

"I think not," Rico said with a satisfied

grin. "Come here, chuckleheads." He walked away from the other students and pulled another cell phone out of his pocket. "This is the real phone." He looked at Miley. "Now you're going to plant one right here," he said, pointing to his face, "or I'll press SEND and everybody will know your precious little secret."

"Miley, just close your eyes. It'll be over before you know it," Lilly said.

Miley felt trapped. She looked from Lilly to Rico and back again. "No, it won't," she said slowly. "It'll never end. He'll hold this over me for the rest of my life."

"Oooh, passion *and* brains," Rico said.

But Miley had come to a decision. Giving up her regular life as Miley Stewart would be hard, but it was better than being blackmailed forever.

"Listen, shrinky-dink," Miley said, moving

in front of Rico, "go ahead, send the picture. But if you think you're going to impress anybody at this school, you're wrong. Sure, they'll know my secret. But they're also gonna find out what a pathetic loser you are." Miley crossed her arms, determined to stand her ground. "So press SEND. Nothing can be worse than this."

Rico locked eyes with Miley, and then sadly flipped his phone closed. He handed it to her with a sigh. "Here. You win."

"Really?" Miley asked. Could it really be this easy, or did Rico have another trick up his sleeve? she wondered.

"Yeah, it's just that I've always been the youngest kid in my class, and the smallest, and just once I wanted to fit in, to be cool," Rico explained.

Rico's speech even made Lilly sympathetic. "Awwww," she said, laying her head on Oliver's shoulder. But then she sniffed and quickly stepped away. "You smell like wet monkey."

Oliver glared at her.

But Miley's attention was still focused on Rico and his explanation.

"And to get a girl like you to kiss me, well, that would've been the coolest thing ever," he said sadly. He hung his head and started to trudge away.

Miley sighed. "Rico, hold on."

Rico turned toward her.

"You know, if you'd just been this real with me from the beginning, things might've been different."

"You mean you would've kissed me?"

"I'm not talking major lip-lock, but a little cheek action? Sure," Miley said. "When you treat people nice, Rico, they're going to treat you nice back. As a matter of fact . . ." Miley smiled and handed Lilly the phone.

"Come here, handsome," she said loudly, getting the attention of the kids on the quad. She picked Rico up and stood him on a picnic bench. They were almost eye-to-eye. "Because you know I can't resist you."

Everybody watched while Rico offered his cheek for a kiss. Miley smiled, puckered up, and leaned in. At the last second, Rico turned his head, grabbed Miley's face, and planted one right on her mouth!

Shocked, Miley pulled back, sputtering. The kids on the quad started to laugh.

Rico pumped his fists in triumph. "Yessss! He shoots! He scores!"

"He's toast!" Miley grumbled.

Rico burst out laughing and took off.

"You'd better run, pal!" Miley cried, racing after him.

"Wow," Oliver said. "I've never seen her so mad."

Lilly was checking out Rico's cell phone. "Oh, yeah? Wait till she sees what Rico thought was her big secret."

Oliver leaned over. Rico's "evidence" was a picture of Miley kissing the teddy bear she had hidden in her backpack. He didn't know about Hannah Montana at all!

Upstairs, Rico raced down the hallway. "Help, monkey, help!" he yelled as he ran past his locker.

The monkey knew what to do. The locker door flew open. Just as Miley came tearing down the hall, the monkey threw a banana peel in her path. The next thing Miley knew, she was flying toward the floor.

Hannah Montana's secret was safe, but Rico had definitely made a monkey out of Miley Stewart.

Put your hands together for the next Hannah Montana book . . .

On the Road

Adapted by Kitty Richards

Based on the series created by Michael Poryes and Rich Correll & Barry O'Brien

Based on the episode, "Get Down Study-udy-udy," Written by Andrew Green

Another amazing Hannah Montana concert was coming to an end. Miley Stewart, wearing her long, blonde Hannah wig, danced along with two of her backup dancers as she belted out the last lines of her hit song "Nobody's Perfect."

When Miley was through, she stood in front of the audience as they cheered and cheered. Looking out into the crowd, she spotted a WE ♥ U HANNAH sign. She grinned. Her fans were too much! She knew that she was, without question, the luckiest pop star on the planet—with the greatest fans ever.

"Thank you! You guys rock!" Miley cried. "Keep on listening, and I'll see you guys when I get back from my very first European tour!" The crowd roared. "I know! I can't wait!" She began to list all her favorite European things: "Swiss chocolate, Italian shoes, and French boys!" She smiled. "Ooh, la la!"

Miley's dad, Mr. Stewart, stood in the wings wearing his manager's disguise, complete with itchy, fake mustache. He frowned. French boys? He didn't think so! "Ooh, la la, uh-uh-uh," he told a stagehand as he crossed off part of Hannah's itinerary. "The closest she's coming to Paris is Paris, Texas!"